The Goalie Mask

by Mike Leonetti

illustrations by Shayne Letain

RAINCOAST BOOKS

Vancouver

Raincoast Books acknowledges the ongoing financial support of the Government of Canada through The Canada
Council for the Arts and the Book Publishing Industry Development Program (BPIDP); and the Government of British
Columbia through the BC Arts Council.

Edited by Scott Steedman and Simone Doust
Interior and cover design by Teresa Bubela

NATIONAL LIBRARY OF CANADA CATALOGUING IN PUBLICATION DATA
Leonetti, Mike, 1958–
      The goalie mask / Mike Leonetti, author; Shayne Letain, illustrator.

ISBN 1-55192-703-9 (bound).—ISBN 1-55192-763-2 (pbk).

      1. Hockey—Goalkeeping—Juvenile fiction. 2. Plante, Jacques, 1929-
—Juvenile fiction. 3. Hockey goalkeepers—Juvenile fiction. I. Letain, Shayne II. Title.

PS8573.E58734G63 2004   jC813'.54   C2004-901959-7

LIBRARY OF CONGRESS CATALOGUE NUMBER: 2004092416

Raincoast Books   *In the United States:*
9050 Shaughnessy Street   Publishers Group West
Vancouver, British Columbia   1700 Fourth Street
Canada   V6P 6E5   Berkeley, California
www.raincoast.com   94710

Acknowledgements
The writer would like to thank Peter Bonanno for the original research material he provided to the author, and Maria
Leonetti for her assistance in reviewing the text for this story. The books of the following authors were used in research:
Tom Adrahtas, Tom Cohen, Jim Hunt, Douglas Hunter, Andy O'Brien, Frank Orr, Raymond Plante, Jacques Plante and
Lorne Worsley. Magazines and newspapers consulted: *Hockey Illustrated, Hockey News, Hockey Pictorial, Sports Illustrated,
Toronto Star,* and *New York Times.* The comic book *The Man Behind the Mask* by *True North Comics* was also used as reference
material. Television documentary viewed: *The Man Behind the Mask* (Great North Productions Inc. for History Television).

Printed in China by WKT Co. Ltd.

10 9 8 7 6 5 4 3 2 1

It was a crisp Saturday morning in October and Grandpa was driving me to hockey practice. It wasn't very far to the arena, but my mind was miles away. I was thinking about how much I loved playing hockey, and especially how much I **loved** being a goaltender. And I was thinking about my coach, Mr. Dumont. He and I didn't always agree on the best goaltending style, and I wasn't sure how to deal with that.

Grandpa noticed that I was lost in thought. He turned to me and said, "Is there something **bothering** you, Marc?"

"No, grandpa," I replied. "I was just thinking about my team. Thanks for taking me to practice." I was trying to **change the subject**.

My Dad used to be a goaltender, and he was really happy when I told him I wanted to become one, too. One of the things I loved about it was all the special equipment, like the **huge** pads. And the blocker and catching glove were so different from the gloves worn by other players. It was fun getting dressed before the game. I loved putting on my mask just before I went into the net. I had covered it with cool stickers with the logo of my favourite team, the **Montreal Canadiens**.

When you are in net, you are always in the middle of the action and everybody is watching when you make a big save! When the game starts, a goalie has to forget about everything else and just concentrate on stopping the puck. I would do **anything** to stop a shot, including diving across the net. I was a pretty good goalie and I liked the way the team counted on me. At practice, I worked on my backwards skating and on catching the puck with my glove hand.

The one part of my game that I really needed to improve was **handling the puck** outside the crease. All the NHL goalies could stop the puck, then pass it right away to a teammate. I tried to do that too, but I was **so bad** at it that Mr. Dumont had told me I had to stay in net and not touch the puck at all! I didn't think that was fair. I **knew** I could be a better goalie if I just practiced more and improved my puck handling.

The next day, I asked Dad if he could play a little ball hockey with me. "Sorry, Marc, but I'm really busy," he replied. "But why don't you ask your Grandpa? He used to be a **goalie too**, you know!"

Grandpa had only just moved in with us, since Grandma died in September. He used to live miles away, so I had only really seen him at Christmas, and didn't know him that well. I certainly didn't know that he used to be a goalie! I raced downstairs to ask him if he wanted to play.

He was a bit slow on his feet, but it turned out that Grandpa had a pretty good wrist shot. And he knew **a lot** about being a goaltender. He showed me how to play the angles, and talked to me about how important it was to bounce right back up after I made a save. That way I'd be ready to stop the next shot.

After an hour of practicing with Grandpa, I was **exhausted** and my Canadiens sweater was soaked in sweat. But I really felt like I was learning new skills.

"Keep it up like that, Marc, and you'll be the next **Jacques Plante!**" Grandpa joked.

I had no idea who he was talking about, but I smiled anyway.

After school the next day, a couple of my friends came over to play hockey in our driveway. I put on my Dad's old pads and we set up a net. Pierre and Denis took turns firing the tennis ball at me and I tried to stop **every shot**.

Just then my grandfather pulled up in his car. He smiled as he watched us play. "Good save, Marc!" he said as I snared a shot with my catching hand.

"Can I ask you a question, Grandpa?"

"Sure, Marc. What is it?

"Who is that Jacques Plante you mentioned the other day? Was he a **famous goalie?**"

He smiled. "Have you boys got a few minutes?"

My grandfather had a great way of telling a story and the three of us stopped playing to give him our complete attention.

M. Richard

H. Richard

J. Béliveau

D. Harvey

B. Geoffrion

D. Moore

J. Plante

"I grew up in Montreal so the Canadiens have always been my team. They used to win the Stanley Cup every season and they had so many great players, like Maurice 'Rocket' Richard, Henri Richard, Jean Béliveau, Doug Harvey, Bernie Geoffrion and Dickie Moore. But my **hero** was Plante because he was a goaltender just like me," my grandfather began.

Pierre turned to me and said with a laugh, "Being a goaltender must run in your family!"

"I guess so," I replied. "Did you follow Plante's career closely, Grandpa?"

"I sure did, Marc. And I'll tell you about the defining moment of his career and how it became one of the **great events** in hockey history."

The three of us were now listening very closely, hanging on to Grandpa's every word.

"I remember that night like it was yesterday. I can still recall the date:

November 1, 1959. I was in New York on business, and we

had just closed a big deal. My boss was so happy with me, he bought us close-up

seats at Madison Square Garden. He knew I was a big hockey fan,

and Montreal was in town to play the New York Rangers.

"The atmosphere in the Garden was amazing. There were only six teams back then — 'The Original Six': Montreal, Toronto, New York, Chicago, Detroit and Boston. And the Canadiens were the greatest. They came to New York as champions — they had won the last four Stanley Cups in a row! The New York crowd was pumped up hoping their Rangers could pull off a big upset. They really wanted to beat the champs from Montreal.

"We cheered all the Montreal stars as they came onto the ice. But the player I was most excited to see was Jacques Plante. When he skated over to the Canadiens net, my boss turned to me and said, 'there's Jake the Snake.'"

We all laughed. "Why did they call him that?" asked Pierre. It seemed like a pretty crazy nickname.

"Because he was so quick and agile, he could throw out a glove or pad or just use his stick to make a save!" answered Grandpa. "He was always diving in all directions, twisting his body like a snake — anything to keep that puck out of the net! He had won four Vezina trophies in a row. In those days, they gave the award to the goalie that allowed the fewest goals in a season."

"So the game started, and it wasn't long before the Canadiens faced disaster. It was still early in the first period when Andy Bathgate, the Rangers big star, picked up a loose puck and came hurtling down the ice. His eyes narrowed, and he let go a high, hard backhand shot. The puck kept rising and Plante could not react fast enough. It hit him square in the middle of his face. And he wasn't wearing a mask!" My grandfather was getting really excited, as if he were still there, doing the play-by-play of the game.

"No mask!" I exclaimed. "How could he play without a mask?"

"Well, believe it or not, in those days the players didn't wear helmets, and goalies didn't wear masks. Coaches thought that a mask would block the goalie's view and he wouldn't see the puck. And a lot of people thought that goalies should just be tough and do whatever they could to stop a shot, even if it meant taking a puck in the face."

"But the puck is so hard!" Denis said.

"So what happened then, Grandpa?" I asked. We were still standing in the driveway, but in our minds we were in Madison Square Garden in 1959.

"Well, there was blood everywhere, and Plante had to **leave the ice**. The doctor sewed up the cut around his nose and lip with seven stitches. His face looked pretty bad. We were standing up in the stands for about twenty minutes, wondering what would happen. The crowd was getting restless. They didn't have back-up goalies on the bench in those days, so either Plante played on, or the Canadiens would have to use some **amateur goalie** sitting in the stands! "

"After he got stitched up, Plante told his coach he was not going back out unless he could wear a mask."

"Wow!" I said. "Did the coach let him do it?"

"Toe Blake was the Canadiens coach and he **wasn't too happy** about it but he had no choice. The coach thought the mask might affect his vision but Plante had been using a mask in practice, so he was used to it. The coach relented and told Plante as long as he stopped the puck and the team kept winning, he could wear his mask. It wasn't a beautiful mask like the ones you see today. In fact, it was a pretty simple mask that Plante had designed **himself** out of fibreglass, but it was light and didn't block his vision."

"Did the Canadiens win the game?" I asked.

"The New York fans gave Plante a **standing ovation** when he came back onto the ice with his mask and his sweater all stained with blood. He played great for the rest of the game and made **27 saves** wearing the mask.

The Canadiens won 3-1. We left Madison Square Garden with big smiles on our faces and talked about Plante **all the way** back to Montreal."

"After that, Plante wore the mask all the time and the Canadiens went on a 19-game unbeaten streak. He even got his **first shutout** using the mask against the Maple Leafs a few days later, 3-0 at the Forum. That year the Canadiens won the Cup again, and Plante won his **fifth straight** Vezina trophy.

"Plante became known as the **'Masked Marvel'** because he played so well. Soon other goalies started wearing masks too. Nobody worried about them not seeing the puck properly any more."

"Every goalie wears a mask now," I said.

"Yes, and you can **thank** Jacques Plante for that," Grandpa replied. "Now you boys finish playing your game."

That night, I was still thinking about the great story my Grandpa had told. We turned on **Hockey Night in Canada** and the Canadiens were playing the Maple Leafs. Mom and Dad were upstairs tucking in my sister, so I was watching the game with Grandpa. He had given me a book Plante had written about goaltending and a hockey card he had saved. I asked Grandpa if he had any more stories about Plante.

"You know, Jacques Plante will always be remembered for using the mask, but he also had a lot of **other ideas**," Grandpa said about his favourite player. "He changed the way goalies played the game. Plante was the first goalie to come out of his net to play the puck and the first to signal icing calls. Goalies didn't do that sort of thing! He even wore a **toque** for a while to stay warm in cold arenas, until the coach made him take it off."

"It sounds like he broke all the rules," I said.

"No, Marc," my Dad said, walking into the room. "He really didn't break any rules. He just **believed** in what he was doing, and knew his own abilities. And look how he made the game safer for everyone. Sometimes you don't follow the trends, you set them yourself. That's what Plante did. He knew that wearing a mask would make him a better goalie and that would **help the team** win more games."

I thought about what my Dad had said and knew that he was right. Jacques Plante had the **courage** to stand up for his beliefs. The next day I told my Dad, "Dad, I have to do what Plante did and talk to my coach. If I practice a lot, I can become a much better goalie. But he has to let me come out of the crease and get to those loose pucks. Otherwise, I'll never get better."

"That's a good idea, Marc," said Dad. "Why don't you ask Grandpa to help you out with your puck-handling skills? You can learn a lot from experienced people like Mr. Dumont and your Grandpa. We support you, Marc. But you have to **listen** to what your coach has to say. I can talk to Mr. Dumont if you want me to."

"No Dad, I'll handle it on my own, just like Jacques Plante did with his coach."

I spent the next week doing drills with Grandpa in the driveway. I worked on using my goalstick, trying to place the puck in just the right spots for my defensemen. My next game was on Sunday morning and I **really** wanted to show the coach that I could come out of the crease like a real NHL goalie and pass the puck out of danger if I had to.

At practice on Thursday, I told Mr. Dumont about all the drills I'd been doing and showed him how much **better** I was at handling the puck. He looked impressed, and told me I could leave the net if I felt sure of myself. For once, I was really feeling **confident**.

On Sunday, the whole family came to watch the game. My team won 3-0! I was up and down all game and I was quick to sprawl to make a stop. But I was fast enough to recover and set myself up for another save. I was twisting myself in every way and made some great saves by kicking out my pads. I loved to hear the whomp the puck made when it hit my pads or ended up in my catching glove! A couple of times the puck came skipping down toward me and I shot out of the crease and flicked it away to a defender. The whole time I was thinking, "I'm Jake the Snake, the Masked Marvel!"

My teammates mobbed me after the game and the coach was waiting for me at the dressing room door. He gave me a pat on the back and said, "That was a well-earned shutout, Marc. You played like an all-star out there!"

"Thanks coach. Does that mean I can play my game without you getting upset with me like before?"

The coach smiled at me. "Well, Marc, you keep stopping the puck and everything will be fine. But don't forget that you've still got a lot to learn."

My Grandpa could see me talking to the coach and he gave me a thumbs up. "Okay, coach, I'm willing to learn," I answered. I was feeling like Jacques Plante talking to Toe Blake. Maybe one day I'll be able to play for the Montreal Canadiens, too!

About Jacques Plante

Jacques Plante was born in Shawinigan Falls, Quebec, in 1929. As a boy Plante dreamed of playing goalie for the Montreal Canadiens. His parents didn't have a radio, so the only way Plante could listen to Canadiens games was by standing on a bureau and listening to the broadcast through the ceiling from the man who lived upstairs. He often waited outside arenas and offered his services to any team in need of a goalie. Many took up his offer and a career was born.

Plante's dream came true when he began his career with the Montreal Canadiens in 1952 and he became the Canadiens number one netminder in 1954–55. Plante led the Canadiens to five straight Stanley Cups between 1956 and 1960, and won the Vezina Trophy as the goalie who allowed the fewest goals five consecutive times during those years. In 1962, he was named the NHL's best player, winning the Hart Trophy to go along with another Vezina. He shared another Vezina Trophy with Glenn Hall when they played together in 1968–69 for the St. Louis Blues.

Plante played for the Toronto Maple Leafs between 1970 and 1973 and had the NHL's best goals-against-average of 1.88 in 1970–71. He also played with the New York Rangers, the Boston Bruins and the Edmonton Oilers (in the World Hockey Association) during his career. His NHL totals include 435 wins and 82 shutouts in the regular season and 71 victories and 14 shutouts in the playoffs. Plante will be remembered as one of the most significant goalies in the history of the NHL. He was elected to the Hockey Hall of Fame in 1978 and died in 1986 at the age of 57.